D1567158

Moritz Petz, alias Udo Weigelt, was born in Hamburg, Germany. Upon completion of his studies, he traveled through Italy, Denmark, and Sweden, working a variety of jobs before returning to study history and German. Today Udo Weigelt lives as a freelance writer on Lake Constance.

Amélie Jackowski was born in Toulon, France. She studied at the School of Applied Arts in Strasbourg and at the University of Aix-en-Provence. The illustrator now lives and works in Marseille. She has two children to whom she likes to tell stories she invented.

Collect the whole series!
The Day Everything Went Wrong
The Bad Mood
Badger is Bored!

Copyright © 2022 by NordSüd Verlag AG, CH-8050 Zürich, Switzerland.
First published in Switzerland under the title *Der Dachs hat heute Langeweile!*
English translation copyright © 2022 by NorthSouth Books, Inc., New York 10016.
Translated by Marshall Yarbrough.

All rights reserved.
First published in the United States, Great Britain, Canada, Australia, and New Zealand in 2022
by NorthSouth Books, Inc., an imprint of NordSüd Verlag AG, CH-8050 Zürich, Switzerland.

Distributed in the United States by NorthSouth Books, Inc., New York 10016.
Printed in Latvia, by Livonia Print, Riga

ISBN: 978-0-7358-4479-7
1 3 5 7 9 · 10 8 6 4 2
www.northsouth.com

FSC
www.fsc.org
MIX
Paper from
responsible sources
FSC® C002795

Moritz Petz | Amélie Jackowski

Badger
Is Bored!

North
South

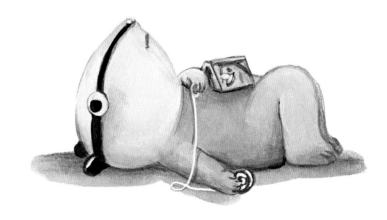

"Oh, brother," thought Badger at breakfast, "I am so bored! I'm more bored than I've ever been before—ever! What should I do? I can't think of a single thing. What if it stays like this forever?"

Badger sighed.

"Okay," he thought, "what do I like to do most?

Oh, I know! Paint! I can paint a nice, pretty picture."

He got started right away.

But it wasn't as much fun as it usually was.

"It's just no use!" groaned Badger at last.

"I am so, so bored!"

Just then there was a knock at the door. Outside was Fox.
Badger was relieved—Fox always thought of something.
But then Fox said, "Badger, you've got to help me! I'm so
bored! Do you have any ideas?"
"Argh!" thought Badger. But then something occurred to him.
"Hey, you really like to build things!" he cried.
"That's true," said Fox, "but today I don't much feel like it
and . . ."
"None of that!" said Badger. "You're going to build a den.
C'mon! I'll help you."

And so they built a den. But today it wasn't exciting. They were glad when Squirrel came over to visit. Of course, Squirrel didn't have any ideas for what they could play either, but now Fox did. "It's so simple!" he said. "You just love to do puzzles!"
"Sure," said Squirrel, "but somehow today I really just don't . . ."
"Nonsense," Fox interrupted, "you're going to do a puzzle! We'll help you."

And so they started working on a puzzle.
Only today the puzzle was so boring that
they were happy when Raccoon came by.
Raccoon's favorite thing to do was to play cards.
And even though he actually didn't feel like
it today, he played a hand with them.
But the boredom still wouldn't go away.

Finally Blackbird and Rabbit came over to Badger's house. Blackbird led the others in a song, though without much enthusiasm. And everyone worked on some crafts, because that's what Rabbit most liked doing. But none of them had much fun. Not even Rabbit, even though he ended up with a nice pinwheel.

"This is the most boring day in my whole life!" complained
Squirrel. "And I bet tomorrow is going to be even more boring!"
"Oh, here you all are."
The animals looked around, and suddenly there was Mouse.
"What happened to you?" asked Badger, surprised.
"It's not as bad as it looks!" said Mouse. "I just hurt myself a
little, so now I have to wear an eye patch for a few days and . . ."
"And actually, now Mouse looks like a pirate," Rabbit said.
"That's it!" cried Badger. "Mouse will be a pirate princess!"
"And we'll need a pirate ship!" cried Fox.

And just like that they all got right to work. Fox, Rabbit, and Squirrel built the ship. Badger drew a treasure map, and Raccoon made a pirate flag. Blackbird came up with a pirate song. And Deer, who had just come by, helped Mouse bake some cookies.

As soon as the animals set out to sea, the wild pirate adventures began.
First they had to fight off a sea monster that was jealous of the princess. But one look at their scary pirate flag and the monster quickly fled back to its cave.

Now a real storm kicked up, so the animals sang a grisly pirate song, and the storm decided he'd better go off and do his storming somewhere else.
After that they used their map to search for buried treasure. When they finally found it, they loaded it on board and set sail for home.

Back home at Badger's house they all gobbled up their
treasure cookies.
"Well, I don't think we'll ever be bored again," said Deer.
Right away the animals started talking about what they
would play tomorrow. And they had so many ideas that
they were sure to have enough for a whole week.

When it was time for Badger to go to bed, he
thought about reading a book. But he was too tired.
"And what will I do tomorrow?" he thought instead.
"Oh, I know! I'll make a picture book about how we
were pirates. Then we'll all be able to think back on
this day whenever we want. And that old boredom . . .
it can go be boring somewhere else. But not
around us!"

what the animals are going to play tomorrow . . .

Mouse is going to make some pretty bracelets.

Fox is going to play hide-and-seek.

Rabbit is going to write Bear a letter.

Squirrel is going to play dress-up.

Raccoon is going to play with play dough.

Blackbird is going to paint stones.

Deer is going to make a collage.